ISBN-13: 978-0-8249-5635-6

Published by Ideals Children's Books
An imprint of Ideals Publications
A Guideposts Company
Nashville, Tennessee
www.idealsbooks.com

Library of Congress CIP data on file

Printed and bound in China

Leo_Jun11_1

She walks a bit
stooped over and wears
a long black dress.
And underneath
her pointy hat,
her hair's a
stringy mess!

The old woman, Miss Fiona,
lives here with all her cats.
A horse and cow live in the barn,
along with several bats.

Now, legend says Fiona
is four hundred years and three,
though she never looked
much older than
two hundred years to me!

In the garden
there's a scarecrow
with his stuffing falling out.
And everywhere you look,
stray cats are lying all about.

This house appears deserted,
but it still is occupied
(although some think its occupants
can disappear and fly)!

Down past the spooky graveyard
and across the stubbled fields,
there lies a big, old haunted house
where all the paint has peeled.

The shutters on the windows
hang crooked, if at all.
The roof is in such bad repair,
it looks about to fall.

Miss Fiona's STUPENDOUS PUMPKiN PiES

Written by Mark Kimball Moulton
Illustrated by Karen Hillard Good

ideals children's books, Nashville, Tennessee

Some folks think she's kooky,
dressed like a witch
on Halloween,
but that just proves
appearances aren't always
what they seem.

For she keeps a tidy garden
with a good-sized
pumpkin patch,
and every Halloween
she serves fresh pumpkin pie
from scratch.

Pumpkins line her
windowsills and
pumpkins line her floor—
she has so many pumpkins,
some come rolling
out the door!

She keeps pumpkins in
her attic and some
in her woodshed.
There are even some
who'll tell you she keeps
pumpkins in her bed!

Then, on the day of
Halloween, and not
one day before,
Fiona gathers all her
pumpkins and begins
her yearly chore.

She hangs a cauldron
on the fire
to bubble and to boil.
She chops and peels
and rolls and stirs
in a frenzied baking toil.

Now and then she'll cackle
as she checks her recipe;
then she'll peek
over her shoulder
to make sure no one sees.

For her ingredients
are secret;
but as she sets
each pie to cool,
the spicy scent that fills the air
makes everybody drool!

Fiona shrieks in welcome,
and we wave and smile to greet her.
Then she slowly lets her spooky gaze
fall on one special trick-or-treater.

She points and crooks her finger
and wiggles her eyebrows,
then cackles:

"Come, my dearie, I need
help inside my house."

This year it's a pink rabbit
who is Miss Fiona's choice.
We all look at her with envy—
all the little girls and boys.

For it's quite the supreme honor
to help Fiona serve her pies—
a most distinguished, rare accomplishment,
to be so recognized.

As angels, spooks,
and goblins start to
gather in the street,
the night is filled with
laughter and the cries of
"Trick or treat!"

Black cats and ballerinas
run to each house
and in-between,
wishing every witch and ghost
a "Happy Halloween!"

But the last house
that we visit, as the midnight
hour draws nigh,
is down past the spooky
graveyard for a slice
of pumpkin pie!

The seconds tick by slowly. . . .
The anticipation grows. . . .
The moon peeks out behind the clouds.
The wind begins to blow.

Then, far off in the distance,
the church bells begin to peal,
and from inside her kitchen,
we hear Miss Fiona squeal.

"Oh, come, all you Witches;
Come Clowns and pirates too!
Come celebrate this Halloween,
and bring your
friends with you!"

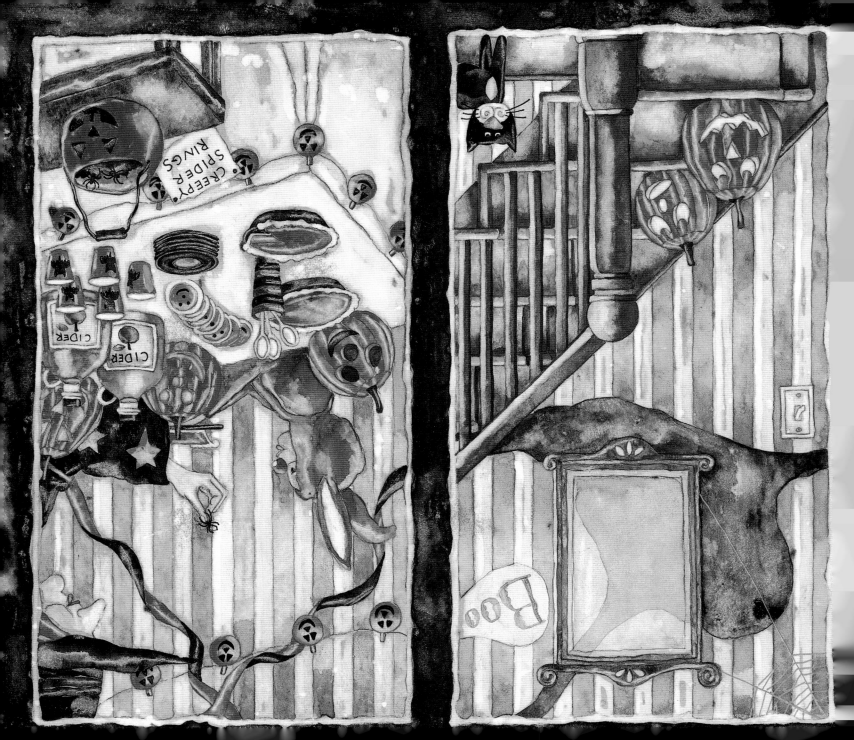

With that, Fiona's helper
throws the front door open wide
and beckons every girl and boy
to come and step inside.

The house is warm and cozy,
with carved pumpkins everywhere.
(Though you must be very careful
not to get cobwebs in your hair.)

The pies are most delicious,
and after we've been fed,
she tells us spooky stories
that make our eyes pop
from our heads!

And as we leave, she sends us home
with an extra slice of pie
for Mom and Dad and Grandma,
who wait up till we arrive.

I must admit, Fiona's kooky,
with her warts and pale green skin.
But who cares how kooky someone looks,
when there's goodness deep within?

Still, I scratch my head and wonder
when folks ask the secret to her pie—
'cause she'll wink and snort and cackle,
to everyone's surprise:

"Just take one big, plump,
ripe pumpkin;
add a lizard and a toad.
Stir in
a few
good
bat
wings...